I'm Maya, and
I want to be a karate kid!

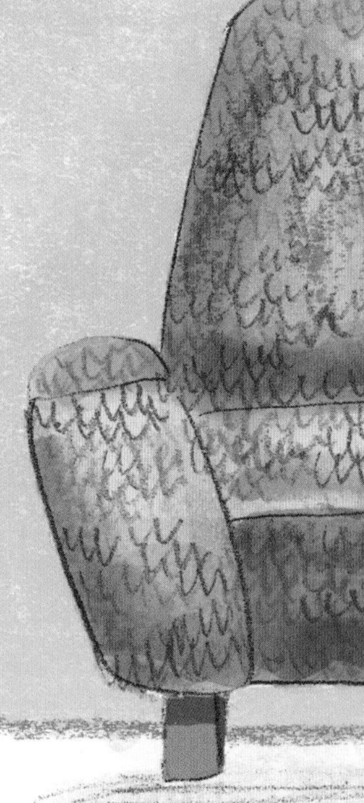

First published 2020 by Walker Books Ltd, 87 Vauxhall Walk, London SE11 5HJ • This book has been typeset in Intro Regular Alt • Printed in China
 British Library Cataloguing in Publication Data: a catalogue record for this book is available from the British Library • ISBN 978-1-4063-8623-3 (hb) ISBN 978-1-4063-9444-3 (pb) • www.walker.co.uk • 10 9 8 7 6 5 4 3 2 1

KARATE KIDS

HOLLY STERLING

WALKER BOOKS
AND SUBSIDIARIES
LONDON • BOSTON • SYDNEY • AUCKLAND

Today I wake up bright and early.
It's Saturday, which means …
it's karate class!

I wear my crisp white suit called a **gi**.

I find my white belt (for beginners like me).

And I'm ready. Let's go!

Dad takes me to the **dojo**.
That's where we practise our karate moves.

All my karate friends are
on their way, too...

Hi, Finja and Patrick!
Hello, Matthew and Hana!
Hey, Pranav!
Hi, Maya!

First, we take our shoes
and socks off.

One ...

and two!

Then we bow to our **sensei**.
She's our teacher.

Sensei asks us to warm up our bodies
from the tops of our heads
to the tips of our toes.

Finja bends down.
Patrick jumps up.

Hana swings her arms
from side to side.

I can't touch my toes yet,
but I stretch as far as I can go.

Then we practise our blocks.

Age uke
blocks our heads.

Soto uke
blocks our stomachs.

And **gedan barai**
blocks down low.

I get a little muddled up with my arms, but Sensei is there to give me some extra help.

Well done,
Maya!

Now it's **kata** time.
This is when we try to remember
a whole pattern of moves.
Who can show me their best stance?

I'm excited to show off
my balance.

But I start to wibble ...
wobble ...

and

bump!

Want some help?
I've got it now, thanks!

When Sensei says "**Yoi**",
I know it's time to show her
what I've got.

I find my balance,
I focus ahead,
and I take a deep breath...
Yoi!

HAI-YAH!

I **kiai** at the top of my voice.

Look, I'm a karate kid!

HAI-YAH!
HAI-YAH!
HAI-YAH!

We all are!

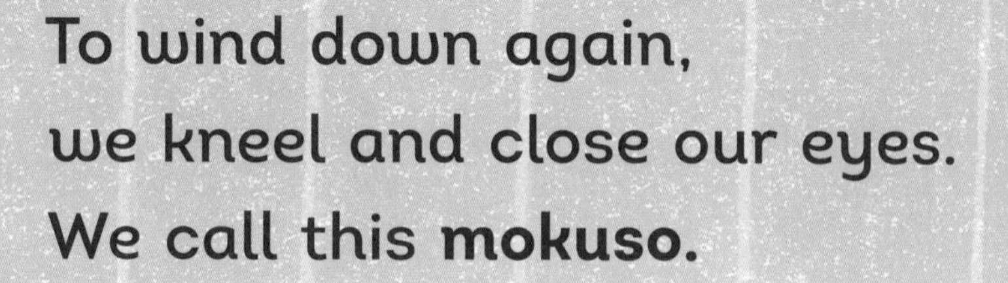

To wind down again,
we kneel and close our eyes.
We call this **mokuso.**

We breathe in ...
and out ...
calmly and slowly.

In ... out.
In ... out.

Whoa! Everyone is here to pick us up already. Karate class always goes so quickly.

Goodbye, Sensei!
See you next Saturday,
karate family!
Bye,
Maya!

As I leave the dojo,
I see Tomoko, one of the big kids,
practising her kata.
She is smooth and graceful.
She has a black belt!

Oh, I really want to be as good
as she is when I grow up...

And maybe I will be.

Hello!

I began karate when I was ten years old. Soon I was taking part in karate competitions all over the world, winning medals at both the European and world levels. In 2013, I became the first female athlete to be crowned Grand Champion two years in a row at the Karate Union of Great Britain's National Championships.

I have now retired from competitive karate, but I teach at my own dojos, and the children whom I have taught over the years have inspired the characters in this story. There is nothing that I love more than teaching. Karate not only helps to improve fitness and flexibility, but it also teaches confidence, mindfulness, compassion and respect. It's also a great way to make friends!

To all those karate kids out there, keep challenging yourself! And to those about to go to their first karate class, I look forward to welcoming you to the karate family!

J Sterling